WE REMEMBER

Written by
Cassie Brooks

Illustrated by
Vaishnavi Dukhande

Dedication

For my mom, who left this world too soon. I wish I had the chance to get to know you better. And for my dad, whose strength lives on in me long after you are gone, your memory is always a part of me.

For Wanda, beloved mother, and Gigi, your love and spirit will always be a guiding light in the lives of those who knew you.

Your memories live on in our hearts and in the stories we tell, shaping who we are. We remember you with love and gratitude, always.

Copyrights

This is a Cassie Brooks book Published by Cassandra Brooks

CB

cassandra.r.brooks@gmail.com

Illustrated by Vaishnavi Dukhande
vaishnavibdukhande@gmail.com

Library of Congress Cataloging-in-Publication Data is available.

#ISBN 979-889480085-1 Printed and bound in the United States
First Edition 2024

"Mom, I miss Gigi." Elijah said, walking into the living room.

"I know, Sweetie," she said, looking up at him.

"I wish she was still here," he sighed.

"I do too," Mom said, watching him with a concerned expression. "A part of her will always be with you."

""How?" Elijah slumped into the sofa.

"She's a part of you. You will always carry her in your heart," she explained.

"Sometimes I forget though," he sighed, folding his hands in his lap.

"That's why we remember her throughout the year." His mom looked at him. "On Samhain, we light candles and have a special dinner, and we remember her around her birthday."
Elijah nodded his head. "Yeah, I know."
"We even created a memorial for Gigi right here in our home." His mom got up led him to a shelf with pictures, a folded flag, and some medals. "You can visit this anytime, but the important thing is to remember her here." She placed her hand over his heart. "As long as we remember her, she never truly leaves us, and if we share her stories, she stays with us for a while too."

Elijah stared intently at the pictures on the shelf. "She loved you very much," she continued. "That's something that can never be taken away from you. Dying is a part of life, and while it is scary for those that we love, we can keep their memory alive by remembering those moments they made us smile or feel loved. Hold onto that, and they will always be a part of you."

"What happens when we die?" Elijah asked suddenly, looking back at her.

"Sometimes our bodies get very old or sick, and it becomes impossible for them to keep going. Other times, accidents happen, but when we die, our souls leave our body and move onto the next life."

"Will she remember me?" Elijah asked.

"She will carry every memory of you with her," his mother explained. "And at certain times of the year, you can call her to you."

"Like a ghost?"

"Not exactly." His mother pulled away and moved in front of him. "Close your eyes and be still."

Elijah went stood unnaturally still and closed his eyes. It was hard for him to do since he wanted to move, and just as he thought he might, he stopped when he suddenly saw his Gigi in his mind.

He remembered being with her at the aquarium. She stood next to him with he peered over a pool with manta rays. His fingers dipped below the water's surface and something smooth and rubbery brushed against his finger tip. His hand whipped out of the water with an excited to trill. When he looked back at his Gigi, she laughed with a broad smile "Good job, Elijah."

Elijah sniffed slightly at the sudden memory, and he could feel his mom's hand back on his shoulder. "I remembered her."

"She loved you very much." His mom said gently. Elijah's reached up and curled his fingers around his mom's hand. "Whatever you do, hold onto that feeling – those memories – and carry them in your heart."

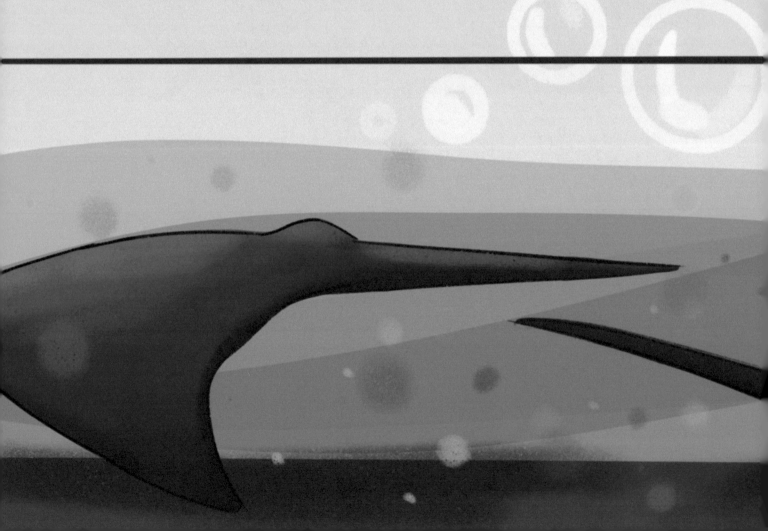

"Does it hurt to die?" Elijah asked softly.
"No, death doesn't hurt. The pain comes before, but when someone dies, they are no longer in pain. Your soul moves on to a place full of love and light where nothing hurts anymore."
"So she's gone gone? I won't see her again?"

"Her body is gone, and her soul has moved on to the next life or perhaps onto Summerland or the Dreaming Place or any other name given for the afterlife."

"Do we have to wait until Halloween to remember her?"
"Halloween is for candy and costumes. Samhain is when we celebrate and honor our loved ones in a special way. But we can do something else too." His mom had an idea and asked them to meet her outside.

"Dad?" Elijah opened the door to his office. "Mom said for us to meet us outside."
"Alright, just a second," his father said. Elijah watched him shutting down the computer before they went into the backyard.

When the went into the backyard, the sun was already low in the sky, and it would be dark soon. He didn't mind the dark, especially when he got to sit with outside with his mom under the moon and the stars and listen to her stories.

His mom had a blanket on the grass with paper and markers waiting for them. "Make yourselves comfortable" she said, as they sat on the blankets. She then handed him some paper. "Draw something that reminds you of Gigi or write a special message."

Elijah drew stick figures of his family and a manta ray from the aquarium with Gigi. He wrote, 'I love you Gigi' and added a heart. "Finished," he said, holding up his paper.

"Excellent," his mother beamed. She folded his paper and instructed him to put glue on it. "Now take this flameless candle and set it on top of your cardboard with your lantern over it."

His drawings glowed softly in the candlelight. The sky grew darker as the sun continued to set. Elijah clutched his paper lantern, eyes wide with anticipation. The soft glow of the lantern reflected in his eyes as he looked up at his parents.
"Mom?" Elijah asked.

"That's perfect," she smiled. Moving closer to the water's edge, she bent forward and placed her lantern on the water's surface, a flameless light flickering within. "Now your turn." Leaning forward, he placed his in lantern in the water. Elijah made a wish, his eyes squinting in concentration, then gently released the lantern. His father knelt beside him, as he did the same.

Elijah watched them all join together in the center of the pond, each lantern decorated with words and pictures of family that had passed. A gentle breeze carried the noises of crickets and frogs, as he watched the lights flicker and cast a small glow on the pond.

As the lanterns danced aimlessly, Elijah saw his parents exchange a smile. His mom stood to her feet a d placed her hand to her heart. "Hail Mom and Dad, I remember." She placed her hand on his shoulder and gently squeezed it.

Elijah stood and leaned into her side. "Gigi, I remember," he said after moment.
The air was filled with a presence of something he couldn't quite explain, but the glow of the lanterns mirrored in the water created a peaceful spectacle, casting a warm, flickering glow on his face and inside of him.

"We remember," his mom said. "We remember," echoed his father's voice. Elijah stepped back in between his parents, and leaned into their embrace. "We remember," Elijah repeated.

The night unfolded with a tapestry of shared stories and laughter and the gentle rustle of lanterns, weaving memories of those long gone that would linger in the hearts of him and his family.

About the Author

Meet Cassie Brooks, the dynamic author behind the award-winning children's book series, "Magick in Me." A talented storyteller and voice of encouragement, Cassie empowers young readers to embrace their individuality. Her picture books, "Sticks and Stones" and "I See the Moon and the Moon Sees Me," carry uplifting messages about celebrating one's unique interests, featuring a young boy named Elijah who learns to stand proud despite others' opinions.

Now residing in Port Richey, FL, with her 9-year-old son Elijah and partner Rob, Cassie draws from her own life challenges to inspire readers. A passionate advocate for the LGBTQIA community, she is dedicated to supporting her neighbors and creating inclusive spaces. Through her writing, Cassie encourages kids to be confident, love themselves, and create their own magick in life.

About the Illustrator

Vaishnavi Dukhande is a self-taught illustrator with a passion for bringing stories to life through vibrant and captivating visuals. She specialises in creating enchanting illustrations for children's books that inspire imagination and foster a love for reading.

Vaishnavi's journey as an illustrator began organically, driven by her love for both art and literature. Without any formal training, she honed her skills through self-study and countless hours of practice. This unique path has allowed her to develop a distinctive style that is both whimsical and engaging, resonating with young readers and igniting their curiosity.

Made in the USA
Columbia, SC
24 October 2024